**Anna Wilson** lives in Northamptonshire with her husband, David, and her children, Lucy and Thomas. She has two black cats called Ink and Jet and a Labrador to match called Kenna. She has written two picture books and plans many more books in the

Nina
Fairy Ballerina series.

 **Nicola Slater** lives in the north of England with Dave the cat. Her work can be seen on books and tablecloths around the globe.

D0993581

Look out for the other books in the

Nina Fairy Ballerina series

New Girl

Daisy Shoes

Best Friends

Show Time

Double Trouble

Coming soon

Party Magic

Dream Treat

Compiled by Anna Wilson

Princess Stories

Fairy Stories

Nina
Fairy Ballerina

Flying Colours

Anna Wilson

Illustrated by Nicola Slater

MACMILLAN CHILDREN'S BOOKS

First published 2006 by Macmillan Children's Books
a division of Macmillan Publishers Limited
20 New Wharf Road, London N1 9RR
Basingstoke and Oxford
www.panmacmillan.com

Associated companies throughout the world

ISBN-13: 978-0-330-44622-8
ISBN-10: 0-330-44622-3

Text copyright © Anna Wilson 2006
Illustrations copyright © Nicola Slater 2006

1 3 5 7 9 8 6 4 2

A CIP catalogue record for this book is available from
the British Library.

Typeset by Nigel Hazle
Printed and bound in Great Britain by Mackays of Chatham plc, Kent

For Mr Phil, who is the only one who knows the Truth About Fairies

Chapter One

Nina was so excited she couldn't keep her feet on the ground. Her mother, Mrs Dewdrop, had invited Peri and Bella to spend the summer holidays with them in Little Frolic-by-the-Stream. It was the last day of their first year at the Royal Academy of Fairy Ballet, and the three fairy friends were in their room listening out for the end-of-term bluebell. Their bags were packed and waiting for them at the gates; they were all set . . .

DRIIING!

"Yipppeee!" cried Bella. "We're off!"

She zoomed out of the door so fast that she left a trail of rainbow sparks behind her as she flew. Peri and Nina laughed at their excitable friend and followed her down to the front of the Academy.

The courtyard was a riot of colour and noise when the friends arrived. Hundreds of fairy ballerinas were milling around, hugging their friends tearfully and calling out to parents who were arriving at the gates to take them home. Swarms of dragonflies were waiting, wings whirring, to speed the fairies away.

"Look, there's your mum, Nina!" Peri shouted above the noise of the fairies' farewells. "Hello, Mrs Dewdrop! Over here!"

Mrs Dewdrop flew up to the gates with Poppy, Nina's little sister.

"Hello, darling!" she cried, giving her eldest daughter a hug. "Are you all ready then, fairies?" she asked, turning to Bella and Peri. Poppy, who liked to be the

centre of attention was
sulking and didn't
even bother to say
hello.

"You bet, Mrs
D!" yelled Peri and she
pirouetted for joy.

"Thanks so
much for letting
us stay," said
Bella. She fiddled
with her hairclips,
feeling shy all of a
sudden. She didn't
know Mrs Dewdrop as
well as Peri did.

"It's going to be
great, isn't it?" Poppy
grumbled. "A whole summer of 'ballet
this, ballet that' – can't wait."

"Now, Poppy dear," her mother
scolded. "Don't start. I've got a surprise
for you all actually."

"What? Is their teacher coming to stay too?" Poppy asked sarcastically.

"No, dear—"

"What is it, Mum?" Nina was bouncing up and down on tiptoes. "Don't keep us in suspense!"

"Your godmother, Heather Pimpernel, has invited us all to go with her to the Festival of Fairy Arts in Asterbury."

Nina looked at her friends, who were both speechless for once, their mouths hanging open. She laughed.

Poppy giggled too, but for quite a different reason.

"A Festival of Fairy Arts!" she squeaked. "You don't want to try saying that in a hurry!"

"Why not?" Nina asked.

Poppy was clutching her sides in hysterics. "You know: Festival of Airy Far—"

"Poppy, really!" her mother cut in irritably.

"Oh, Mum, it's only a joke. Come on, you lot!" Poppy cried, wiping tears of laughter from her eyes. "What are you waiting for? Race you to our dragonfly!"

Chapter Two

The fairies had spent a busy afternoon at Nina's house in Little Frolic deciding what luggage to take to the Festival of Fairy Arts. Mrs Dewdrop explained that the fairies would be camping, so they should not take much with them. They would need practical clothing, so, much to their dismay, they couldn't take their ballet outfits. The fairies looked so disappointed however that Mrs Dewdrop relented a little.

"You can wear whatever you like for the first day," she said.

Nina rushed off to put on her
favourite pink T-shirt with a sparkly
butterfly logo, and a darker pink petal-
skirt.

At last Peri and
Nina went to load their
rucksacks on to
a waiting
dragonfly, but
Bella still
wasn't
ready. While
no one was
looking, she
quietly
took
her
wand and
rapped
out a
quick spell:

I'm Foxy Glove's daughter.
I can't obey
All these rules
Mrs D has given me today.
I need loads of clothes –
I can't pick and choose –
I won't just take some T-shirts,
Shorts and sensible shoes.
So come on, fairy magic,
Help me make more space.
I want glitzy clothes
And party shoes –
In my suitcase!

A blast of light filled the room like a firework, and Bella was thrown to the floor.

"Wow! That spell was more powerful than I thought!" she said, her almond eyes wide as buttercups.

She looked at her rucksack, which was now bulging. But the clasps were still done up and no clothes were falling out.

It seemed as though Bella had got away with a bit of mischievous magic yet again.

The festival was started seventy years ago by the previous fairy queen, Queen Aster, to celebrate all the artistic talent in fairyland. Asterbury was already humming with activity when Nina and her friends and family arrived. They had never seen so many different fairies before. There were musicians and dancers of every kind, as well as fairy actors and fairy acrobats . . . Some of the fairies were already famous throughout all fairyland for their talents.

"Look over there!" Peri cried. "It's McBee!"

"What are you talking about, Peri?" Nina said. Peri was pointing at a group of straggly-haired, moody-looking fairies with guitars slung about their wings.

"Oh, Nina, come on!" Peri shouted,

fluttering
round in crazy
circles. "They're only
the best rock band ever!"

"You don't listen to *rock*
music?!" Nina sounded shocked
at the very thought.

"Not everyone is as obsessed with
ballet as you, Nina," Peri teased.

"Now, fairies," said Mrs Dewdrop,
"I'm sure we're all a little tired after the
journey. Let's pitch our tents and go and
find something to eat. The festival has
some of the best food in fairyland, they

say – cooks come from all over to sell their creations. Ah look – there's Heather. I hope she's saved us a good place to camp."

Nina's fairy godmother had arrived early to save them all a space.

"I thought this would be the perfect spot," she said, once everyone had said hello. "We've got an area where we can have a campfire in the evenings. I've brought my foldaway toadstools too – I thought you'd like that, Cherry," she said to Mrs Dewdrop.

"I love campfires!" Poppy shrieked, zooming into the air in delight. "We can melt marshmallows on it and lob them at passing fairies!"

"Poppy, really!" said her mother in exasperation.

The fairy friends giggled.

"Right, first things first," said Heather, smiling at Poppy. "Let's get the tents up. I'll be sharing with Cherry and Poppy, and you three can stay together in the other one. Put them on the ground and stand back."

Heather raised her wand in the air and called out:

Tents, stand up and take your place.
Make this camp a cosy space!

In a shower of lilac stars, the fabric, poles and ropes stood to attention. They then turned to Heather, bowed, and clicked into place.

The fairies were delighted and clambered in through the tent flap to explore. Everything inside was luxurious and warm – there was soft grass matting on the floor and some plump cushions to sit on. They laid out the cocoon sleeping bags Heather had brought for them.

"This is great, but we'll have loads of time to snuggle up in here later," said Peri. "I don't know about you guys, but I'm desperate to get out there and look around! Come on!"

Chapter Three

Nina and Bella were just as keen to go exploring right away – as was Poppy, but Mrs Dewdrop persuaded her to stay behind to help put the finishing touches to the camp.

"Let those three have some time together first, dear," she suggested. "You can join them later."

Poppy pouted. "And I get to stay here and drink chamomile tea with you as usual, I suppose. How exciting . . . oh, it's not fair!"

Nina beckoned to her friends to leave

before they could get involved in a family argument. Heather had given them a map of the festival, showing all the stalls and tents and listing the names of the artists attending. She had also made sure they knew where the judges' tent was in case of emergencies.

"I know the judges, so if you have a problem, just go there and mention my name," she'd explained kindly.

But problems were the last things on any of the fairies' minds. The festival was full of so many exciting things to do! There were workshops and masterclasses for anyone to join; there was even going to be a competition between the various groups to find the best talent in fairyland. This immediately caught Bella's eye.

"Hey, let's give it a go!" she cried. "We can always use a bit of magic to make sure we win."

"Bella!" Nina was shocked at the idea of cheating.

"OK, OK, I didn't mean it," Bella said huffily.

"Anyway, it'd be hard to cheat," said Peri, who was reading a leaflet about the competition. "It says here in the competition rules that no one may use magic – it's to do with Health and Safety on stage apparently."

Nina was more interested in the workshops.

"Look!" she cried. "Celandine Rosebud, the famous fairy ballerina, is holding a class here. Oh, let's go and sign up for that now!" She went skipping off in the direction of the ballet tent, holding

her skirts out and practising pointing her toes.

"I thought we were meant to be on holiday," Peri protested.

"Don't be a spoilsport, Peri," Bella said, taking her friend's hand. "We wouldn't be here if it wasn't for Nina."

The three fairies leaped into the air and flew through the crowds of hovering festival-goers, with Nina leading.

It was difficult not to be sidetracked on the way – there was so much to look at.

Peri screeched to a halt in mid-air at one point and cried out, "Wow! There's Scarlet Larkspur – she was in that play about the fairy princess who had an enchantment put on her when she pricked her finger on a spindle. Wouldn't you just LOVE to meet a real live actor?"

"Are you going to spend the whole holiday spotting celebrities?" Bella butted in, sighing. "I thought I'd come here to get away from all that. Mum spends her life with all the stars of fairyland—"

"Great! That means you can introduce me to some," Peri retorted.

Nina laughed. "Come on, you two. Let's go and sign up for that ballet class."

I'm not sure I want to do any ballet on holiday, thought Peri. But it didn't look as if she was going to have much choice. "Listen," she said suddenly. "I don't really want to queue all afternoon. Can you put my name down for me while I go and explore?"

"Er – yes, of course," Nina said, frowning. "I suppose that'll be all right. Meet us back at the tent at five o'clock. I'm sure we'll be done by then."

Peri thanked her friends and fluttered away. She had been dazzled by the sight of Scarlet Larkspur; she loved all the plays the actor had been in. I have to try and meet her, she thought. Perhaps I could get her autograph.

Peri whizzed through the air, past the food stalls, and caught sight of the famous actor again. Ms Larkspur was heading towards a silver-and-pink striped tent. Peri followed and noticed a poster by the entrance to the tent:

THE
SHAKESPINDLE PLAYERS

Come and see what an actor's life is like!

WORKSHOPS and **TUTORIALS**

by the famous actor **MS SCARLET LARKSPUR**

open to all festival-goers! Take part in a production of

WILLOW SHAKESPINDLE'S latest play:

A Midsummer's Daydream

"Cool!" Peri breathed. "This I *must* see."

Chapter Four

Nina and Bella reached the front of the queue after a long wait. They could see inside the large ballet tent now: there was a stage at the front and some fairy ballerinas were giving a demonstration.

"They're so graceful!" Nina sighed. "Each movement is so controlled – just look at them, Bella."

Bella nodded. "They make it look so easy, but we all know how tough it is to hold a position without wobbling!" She stood up on tiptoe on her left leg, and pointed her right leg out in an arabesque on demi-pointe – and then promptly fell over in a giggling heap.

"Hmm, someone's got a lot to learn," said a mocking voice. A slim fairy ballerina with a clipboard had appeared beside the two friends. She was wearing a gold leotard with matching tights, leg warmers and ballet shoes. Her curly, jet-black hair was swept off her face in a gold hairband.

"Come to sign up for the masterclass, I guess?" she enquired.

"Oh yes!" Nina cried, clasping her hands together. "I adore Celandine Rosebud and—"

"Don't we all, luvvie, don't we all," the dark-haired fairy

replied. "I'm Zinnia, Celandine's personal assistant. And who are you?"

Bella and Nina nervously told Zinnia their names, and explained that their friend Peri would be joining them too.

Then Bella blurted out, "When do we get to dance?"

"First things first, sweetie. You'll have to go and change," Zinnia said, looking them up and down. Her lips were pursed in disapproval.

Oh why didn't Mum let us bring any ballet things? thought Nina.

"Sorry, but we don't have any—"

"No problem!" Bella butted in. "We'll have our ballet kit on tomorrow, you'll see."

"So you have *danced* before?" Zinnia asked.

"Oh yes," Nina said breathlessly. "We're from the Royal Academy of Fairy Ballet."

Zinnia did not seem impressed. "Off

you go and change and I'll see you back here at nine o'clock tomorrow morning, luvvies," she said as she twirled away to greet the next budding ballerinas in the queue.

"Why did you say 'no problem'?" Nina sounded panicky. "You know we haven't got our ballet stuff."

"Just chill out, Nina. I've got it covered," Bella replied.

Bella and Nina flew back to the tent to meet Peri. Mrs Dewdrop and Heather had already organized a picnic, and Peri was helping build a campfire with Poppy. Heather handed Nina and Bella a buttercup of tea each.

"So, tell us about your afternoon," she said, pulling up a toadstool and sitting down. "Peri says you've signed up for a masterclass already! Can't keep you away from ballet, even on holiday, can we?" she teased.

Nina's blue eyes sparkled as she told her fairy godmother and her mum all about meeting Zinnia, and how Celandine Rosebud was going to teach them the next day.

"We put your name down too, like you asked, Peri," Bella said.

"Er, oh, right," Peri replied hesitantly. "Sounds great."

"So, what did you get up to after you

left us?" Nina asked, nibbling at a seed cake.

"Just rubbing shoulders with the stars, you know—" Poppy piped up.

"No, no, nothing," Peri interrupted, giving Poppy a warning look. "I, er, I just mooched around a bit. Looked at all the stalls, you know. There are some amazing crafts here," she said airily.

"Yes, dears," Mrs Dewdrop chimed in. "I think we should glide around together this evening before the sun sets and take a look at everything. What do you think?"

"Good idea," said Bella. "Then we can come back and set fire to some marshmallows, eh, Poppy?"

Chapter Five

"**W**ake up, Bella! Wake up, Peri!"
Nina cried, giving her friends a
shake.

"Eh? Whassat? Gerroff!" Peri grumbled.
She brushed Nina away and snuggled
down deeper into her sleeping bag.

"Ninaaa!" Bella complained. "It's still
night-time."

"No, it's not," Nina said excitedly.
"It's eight o'clock already, and if we want
to get to Celandine's class on time we'd
better hurry up. And we've got to sort out
some clothes before we get there."

"OK, OK, don't get your wings in a twist," Bella said, rubbing her eyes and running her hands through her dark hair. "Let me at least have a cup of mint tea first."

The fairies sat down to breakfast in their pyjamas, munching muesli and slurping tea as quickly as they could.

"You three are up early," Mrs Dewdrop commented.

"Can't be late for the famous Celandine Rosebud, Mrs D," Bella said, winking.

When they'd finished breakfast, Bella beckoned her friends back into their tent. She held her finger to her lips, then she dragged her rucksack out. Holding her wand over it she whispered a short spell:

Change us out of these gross pyjamas
We look like a right bunch of bananas!
Dress us in leotards and ballet pumps
Celandine Rosebud doesn't like frumps!

ZAP! A blast of white light filled the tent, almost blinding the fairies. They shrieked and staggered backwards. When the light had disappeared the fairies gasped at each other.

"How did you do it, Bella?" Nina asked. She was staring at her two friends who were wearing the most glamorous ballet outfits she had ever seen. Peri was in green from top to toe. Her leotard was shimmering with glitter and

her satin ballet shoes matched. She also
had a little green gauze tutu covered in
tiny silver stars. The clothes seemed to
make her emerald eyes shine even more
brightly than usual. Bella's ballet outfit
was bright pink. There were tiny hearts
glistening on her tights; even her hairclips
were now covered in little hearts.

"You both look like superstars!" Nina
exclaimed. "What do I look like?"

She looked down at
her clothes. She
was dressed in
brilliant blue, the
colour of the sky on
a hot summer's
day. Her tutu
was decorated
with delicate
gold flowers that
brought out the
highlights in her hair.
"You look great,

Nina, as always," said Peri, smiling. "Come on, we really should fly. It's a quarter to nine."

The fairies whizzed off quickly before they had to answer Mrs Dewdrop's astonished questions about where the outfits had come from.

"I think Bella Glove has more than a few tricks under her wings," said Heather to her old friend as they watched the excited trio fly away across the festival grounds.

The three friends went straight into the ballet tent and started warming up as their teacher, Miss Tremula, had taught them. They knew it was important to stretch their muscles before they started any serious dancing, to avoid injuring themselves. They were concentrating on pointing and flexing their feet when a fanfare of trumpets blared out. The fairies stopped in their tracks and turned to face

the tent entrance, where
the music was coming
from. A tall, graceful,
sun-tanned fairy
hovered at the front
of the tent,
surveying the
crowd inside with
a critical eye. She
was wearing a
strapless, deep-ruby-
coloured dress, and her
golden hair was piled up
high on her head in an
elaborate style. Her shiny
red lips matched her
dress; she was wearing a
large ruby on a chain
around her neck, and her
ears were dripping with
jewels.

It was none other than
Celandine Rosebud.

Nina immediately became nervous at the sight of the famous prima ballerina. She looks just like her portrait at the Academy, she thought. Only *much* scarier.

"What's the matter, Nina?" Bella whispered, catching sight of her friend, whose face had gone the colour of Peri's outfit.

"She — she looks terrifying!" Nina stammered.

"Can't be as bad as my mum," said Bella airily. "Come on — it's meant to be fun, remember?"

"Quiet now!" Celandine called out, as she flew to the stage at the front of the tent. "My assistant, Zinnia, tells me that we are honoured to have a few pupils from the Royal Academy of Fairy Ballet here today," she continued, looking at Nina and her friends. She smiled. "Looks like my ballet class will be winning this year's competition with flying colours! So, let's see what you're made of."

Great! thought Nina. A chance to impress a real prima ballerina.

"Right then," Bella muttered to Nina, her almond eyes gleaming. "Let's do what the lady says – I know a trick to spice things up a bit!"

Before Nina could protest, Bella flicked her wand behind her back and – WHOOSH! – the whole class was scooped up into the air by an invisible hand. Immediately they went into a series of dizzying fouettés: whirling round and round on their right legs, their left legs whipping back in a circular movement, making them spin like tops.

"This'll impress her – fantastic, eh?" Bella shouted out to Nina breathlessly.

But the rest of the class had never danced before and didn't share Bella's enthusiasm. They were starting to feel unwell.

"AARGH! Stop!" they cried out to

Celandine, thinking the magic was her doing.

Celandine Rosebud was not amused. Flicking her own wand irritably she shouted above the din:

Stop all this whirling!
Enough of your twirling!

The fairies stopped spinning, and gratefully returned to the ground. Nina was so dizzy she was seeing stars. Celandine frowned at the class.

"That was dangerous," she said. "Has no one ever told you not to try to fly before you can flutter? A ballerina has to learn the basics before attempting anything so complicated—"

"But we didn't do that on purpose!" exclaimed one exhausted fairy.

Peri took advantage of the confusion to edge towards the tent flap. She had had enough. She quickly slipped out while no one was looking and went to find Poppy. I'm not staying to get caught up in Bella's tricks, she thought. Poppy and I have other plans . . .

Chapter Six

Celandine quickly called her masterclass back to order. "There are many other fairies who are keen to benefit from my experience. If you are not going to take this class seriously, I suggest we stop now," she said sternly.

Nina looked around wildly and grabbed Bella by the arm. "Where's Peri?" she hissed. "She's gone!"

Celandine looked suspiciously at Nina and Bella. "Is there a problem? I don't tolerate gossiping in my class, fairies, and

I certainly expect better from pupils of the Royal Academy."

Everyone was now staring at Nina and Bella. Nina looked down at her ballet shoes and muttered an apology, but Celandine ignored her and was already starting to explain her ideas for the competition.

Bella tried to reassure her friend.

"Look, Nina, let's work hard this morning and show Celandine how good we are," she whispered, as she copied Celandine's demonstration of a demi-plié. "We can find Peri later and get her back here this afternoon."

Nina reluctantly agreed. It won't feel right though, dancing without Peri, she thought to herself. However, she was determined not to let it get to her and she quickly found she didn't have time to dwell on Peri's absence. While the others were still practising demi-pliés, Celandine called her and Bella over for a chat.

"I can see that you two are going to get bored if we just concentrate on the basics," the famous ballerina said. "I'll get Zinnia to teach this lot, then you and I can work out some choreography for the competition."

"But won't the others be disappointed?" Nina asked.

"That's very sweet of you, dear," Celandine replied quickly, "but you needn't worry. Remind me, what are your names?"

Bella told her.

"Well, Bella, you and Nina will perform solos and the others will be the chorus — the corps de ballet, as it's known," Celandine explained. "That way, I can concentrate on developing your technique — and it'll be much more fun for me too!"

Celandine Rosebud was obviously a fairy who was used to getting her own way.

The rest of the morning passed in a flash for Nina as she lost herself in the lesson.

They won't believe it back at the Academy when I tell them Bella and I had a private lesson with Celandine Rosebud! Nina thought. I can't wait to tell Peri. What can she be up to? I wonder.

"Now let's get that fouetté right, shall we?" Celandine was saying. "That disgraceful display earlier was not at all how it should be done."

Celandine stood with her feet turned out perfectly. She was so supple that her legs seemed to be at right angles to her hips. Nina knew that only very experienced dancers could turn their legs out so far. Not for the first time, she realized she had a *lot* more to learn before she had a hope of turning professional. She and Bella concentrated on the prima ballerina as she went into

an "attitude" – she stood gracefully on
her right leg, the other leg raised behind
her body with the knee bent. Then she
swiftly kicked out her left leg and
whipped it around in a circle, sending
herself spinning round on her right leg. A
fabulous fouetté! Bella
and Nina felt dizzy
just looking at her.

   "Now it's
your turn, fairies.
Concentrate on
the attitude first,"
Celandine
commanded.
"That's it,
Nina. Lovely
– you have
great poise.
Bella, dear, you
need to think
about being a bit
lighter on your feet.

The ballet term used to describe such lightness is 'ballon' – it comes from the French word for 'balloon'. You need to think of bouncing lightly or floating silently through the air like a little balloon!"

Bella laughed, but had to admit it was a good description.

Nina had soon perfected doing a fouetté once, but found it hard to spin round and round as Celandine had done. She kept seeing stars! Celandine told her a good trick was to find something to look at before she began.

"Fix your eyes on something – try looking at that chair over there. Right, now as you spin round, zip your head back to face the chair . . ." Nina did as she was told. It worked, but she still felt a little dizzy. There are those stars again, she thought.

Celandine was encouraging nevertheless. "Perfect!" she cried. "You see? Once you have something to focus on, you can do it!"

Nina had another go and tried hard to ignore the stars. She concentrated on the chair and this time it *was* easier.

"It's true, Bella!" Nina cried as she whizzed round and round on her right leg, her left leg acting like a mini propeller. "I can do it! You try, Bella."

The two friends were soon spinning round and round together.

With a teacher like Celandine, anything is possible, Nina thought to herself. Perhaps we really could win the festival competition after all!

Chapter Seven

The morning was over all too soon, and Nina and Bella decided to go back to their tent to find Peri and have lunch.

"I really hope Peri's not in a bad mood," Nina said anxiously.

"Yeah," Bella said. "Let's hope she found something fun to do . . ."

When they got closer to their camp they hovered back a little to try to see how Peri looked. She wasn't wearing her beautiful ballet clothes any more – she was back to being the scruffy fairy the friends loved. And they needn't have worried about Peri being cross: on the contrary, she was beaming all over her pretty pixie face and she and Poppy were chattering away like two little sparrows.

"Hi, you two!" Nina called out as she fluttered over. "You look happy."

"Yeah, Peri and I have had the most fantastic morning!" Poppy laughed. "We met—"

Peri nudged Poppy in the ribs.

"All right, all right," Poppy sighed, sticking out her tongue.

"What's going on?" Nina asked.

"Nothing," Peri cut in quickly.

"What are you up to, Periwinkle?" Bella said teasingly. "You flew out of the ballet tent faster than a hummingbird this morning."

"Yeah, I, er . . ." Peri mumbled. "Listen, I know you're not going to like this, Nina, but I don't like Celandine Rosebud. I think she's stuck up and I'd rather not do her class if it's all the same to you."

Nina couldn't believe it.

"Oh, Peri! Look, I know she's strict and a bit scary, but she's the most amazing teacher – Bella and I have learned how to do a fouetté, and—"

"What's a fwettay?" Poppy butted in. "Do you pour buckets of water over each other or something – you know, to get 'Wet, eh'?!"

"Be quiet, Poppy. That's not even funny," Nina snapped. Nina turned to Peri. "Come back with us after lunch," she pleaded.

"I'm sorry, Nina," Peri said. "I'm really happy for you, but I'm on holiday and I want to relax. So I'll just hang out with Poppy. You guys enjoy yourselves, OK?"

It was no good. Nina could see that she wasn't going to convince Peri to come back to the ballet tent that afternoon.

It was the same every day after that: after breakfast Peri would go off with Poppy, and Nina and Bella would go to meet Celandine. It was obvious that Peri was happy spending time with Poppy, and it was nice for Poppy not to be left out, so Nina decided to try to forget about it, and concentrate on her dancing.

The competition day drew nearer, and

the excitement level was mounting around the festival. Wherever the friends flew, they could hear fairies gossiping about the competition and discussing who they thought should win. The competition was to go on all day and end late at night with the prize-giving on the main festival stage.

But on the day before the competition, disaster struck! Nina and her friends were woken by the sound of shouting.

"Liar!" someone shrieked. "I am *not* a cheat! And I *will* win this competition . . ."

I recognize that voice, Nina thought sleepily. She poked her head out of the tent flap to see what was going on.

"Take that for your impudence!" screeched the mystery person.

ZAP! Nina was thrown back into the tent by the force of a sparkling shower of ruby-coloured shooting stars.

"Nina! Are you all right?" Peri

shouted, leaping out of her sleeping bag to help her friend. "What's going on?"

"I – I think there's an argument going on outside!" Nina stammered, trying to get her breath back.

Peri peeped out to see where the kerfuffle was coming from.

POW! This time she was knocked back by a shower of frogs!

"Urgh! Heather! Mrs Dewdrop! Help!" Peri cried. "We're under attack!"

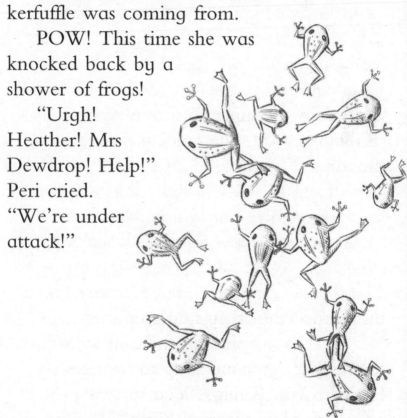

Chapter Eight

Heather Pimpernel was always good in a crisis. She quickly took charge, shouting:

Frogs! Please! Get back in your pond
As soon as I wave my magic wand!

The frogs disappeared and Heather asked the fairies what they had seen and heard.

"There's no one out there now. Still, sounds like someone is up to no good," Heather said grimly. "You saw *ruby-*coloured stars, you say, Nina? Cherry,

make them a nice cup of chamomile
tea with honey – they've had a shock.
Leave this to me, fairies." And she
flittered off.

"Why was Heather so interested in
the colour of the stars?" Nina asked her
mother.

"Oh, you know Heather – she likes a
bit of excitement!" her mother joked.
"I'm sure it's nothing, but it's better to be
safe than sorry. We can't have fairies
throwing frog spells around like that.
Someone could get hurt. Besides, it's not
fair on the frogs, poor things," she added
thoughtfully.

"I've just realized!" Nina cried
suddenly. "I knew I recognized that
voice. And that's why Heather wanted to
know about those stars . . . Wait here.
I've got to find Heather – now!"

Nina remembered what Heather had
told her to do if there was an emergency.
She left her bewildered friends and family

and immediately made for the judges'
tent. Heather said she knew the judges,
Nina thought, so she's bound to have
gone there.

Once inside the judges' tent, Nina
spotted Heather straight away and
landed rather inelegantly right in front
of her fairy godmother, her wings all
crumpled and her hair ruffled.

"Nina? What are you doing here?"
Heather asked, surprised.

Nina explained that she thought she
knew who had cast the frog spell.
Heather said she would introduce Nina
to the judges so that she could tell them
all about it. Some of the judges were old
friends of Heather's and were pleased to
meet her fairy god-daughter.

". . . and I'm sure it was Celandine
Rosebud. She's been teaching me this
week, you see," finished Nina.

"Yes, well, I suspected as much,"
Heather said. "She is the only fairy I

know whose wand produces showers of ruby-red stars . . ."

One of the judges nodded slowly. "All this is very interesting," she said. "Especially in the light of the note we received this morning." The fairy held up a white rose-petal with some tiny loopy writing on it. The note said:

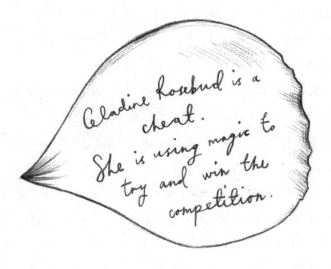

Celadine Rosebud is a cheat. She is using magic to try and win the competition.

"Is this true, Nina?" Heather asked gently.

"It can't be!" Nina cried. "Bella and I have been working really hard!"

Heather put her hand on Nina's shoulder. "I'm sure you have, dear," she said. "But perhaps you've noticed something strange? Does Celandine use her wand in any of her dances? Have you seen any more of those ruby-red stars that you saw this morning?"

Nina nodded slowly, tears trickling down her face. "Yes, I have seen those stars before," she admitted. "Whenever she teaches us a difficult move . . . oh, I thought it was just me feeling a bit dizzy!"

"It's not your fault, Nina," Heather soothed. "We all know you are a brilliant ballerina. No one thinks *you* have cheated. We need to find the author of the note and see if they have anything to add that might help us. Don't cry, dear — we'll sort this out. We can't have the festival ending on a bad note, can we?" she said cheerfully.

Later that day, Heather arrived back at the campsite with a shamefaced Zinnia in tow.

"Zinnia has admitted to writing the note about Celandine," Heather explained.

"It's all true!" Zinnia insisted. "She's only got where she is today by magic. I'm the talented one, but *you* wouldn't know that. I fly around, waiting on her, hand and wing . . ."

"We get the picture," said Heather kindly. "You did the right thing."

"But you won't tell her it was me?" Zinnia asked, panicking.

"No, dear. The judges will make a

general announcement later this evening," Heather said.

"Bella and I are still going to be in the competition, aren't we?" asked Nina.

"That will be for the judges to decide, I'm afraid," said Heather cautiously.

Unfortunately, the judges' announcement was not good news as far as Nina and Bella were concerned. The fairies heard the news that evening when a voice rang out over the loudspeakers:

"Celandine Rosebud and her dancers have been banned from tomorrow's competition, as the No Magic rule has been broken." A murmur went up all over the festival grounds. "All other competitors are to meet at the main tent at nine o'clock to be given a revised schedule."

"I don't believe it!" Bella fumed. "The old bat!"

"I don't care. I'm not letting

Celandine Rosebud ruin my summer holiday!" Nina declared. "We are going to win that competition, Bella. You see if we don't!"

Chapter Nine

Back at the campsite, Bella was still furious. But Peri had come up with a plan.

"Stop flouncing, Bella – you look just like your mum!" Peri teased. "Listen, I've been thinking, maybe you and Nina should join Poppy and me."

Bella looked annoyed. She didn't like being compared to her mother. "What, in the audience?" she snapped. "I think I'd already worked that one out for myself, thanks."

"No, er – oh, Poppy, I think I'm

going to have to tell them, aren't I?" Peri asked nervously.

"Don't ask me," Poppy muttered. "I was going to tell them last time, but you wouldn't let me."

"What are you two going on about?" Nina asked.

"Well, you know that morning that I left you and Bella with Celandine?" Peri began. The others nodded. "I went to see what Poppy was up to."

"Yeah!" Poppy butted in excitedly. "I'd got so bored with Mum and Heather. They droned on and on about what the best time of year for planting sweet peas is . . . blah, blah, blah."

"Anyway," Peri said, glowering at Poppy, "I couldn't find her, but then I caught sight of Scarlet Larkspur again and I got a bit sidetracked . . ."

"You're not making sense, Peri," Nina said gently. "Slow down."

Peri took a deep breath and explained

that she'd followed the famous actress into the drama tent, where a workshop was being held. Scarlet was running the workshop with the writer Willow Shakespindle – and Peri had found Poppy there too! It turned out that the workshop was preparing a short play for the competition called *A Midsummer's Daydream*. Before she knew it, Peri found herself sitting with Poppy, transfixed by Willow's words.

"He's so clever!" Peri breathed. "His ideas are more enchanting than the best fairy magic ever! He's written tons of plays, and all the famous actors in fairyland have starred in them. Anyway, Poppy and I decided to sign up there and then to act in *Daydream*. I'm going to be Tilia, the Fairy Queen—"

"And I'm going to be Bogbean, the naughty sprite!" Poppy cried.

"Bogbean, eh? Yeah, well we're really happy for you," Bella said sarcastically.

"You're just jealous, Boghead!" Poppy taunted.

"Poppy, really!" Nina said, sounding just like her mother. "Why didn't you tell us about this before?" she asked Peri.

"Yeah, and how's this going to help Nina and me dance in the competition?" Bella added.

"Well, I thought you and Bella would tease me if I told you I was having a go at acting," Peri said to Nina shyly. "But listen, I've had an idea. There's this bit in the play where some fairies meet in the forest on Midsummer's Day to cast a spell on the prince," she continued, getting excited again, "and, well, I thought it would be great if the scene was done as a ballet. Scarlet's been teaching us all about the importance of improvisation – that's making stuff up while you're acting – so I'm sure she won't mind you guys joining in. What do you think?"

"Peri, you are a genius!" Nina cried.

"I think it's a fabulous idea. And it will mean we can all perform together too. Oh, well done, Peri. Come on, let's go and ask Willow Shakespindle and Scarlet now."

Even Bella had to agree it was a great idea.

Chapter Ten

Nina and her friends didn't get much sleep the night before the competition. Willow and Scarlet had thoroughly approved of Peri's idea and had set everyone to work right away, planning the choreography. The friends had finally collapsed into their sleeping bags at midnight.

The next morning passed in a whirl of activity. Willow had found some costumes for Nina and Bella. They were made of leaves and petals and were very comfortable to dance in.

"You can dance in bare feet, can't you?" Willow asked them. "It will be more authentic: we want you to look like real wood sprites!"

The final rehearsal went well. Afterwards the fairies went to watch the other acts perform – and to check out the judges.

"Look at that old one with the monocle – she looks terrifying!" Nina whispered to Peri. "She doesn't look very impressed with the band that's just played."

The fairy friends were enjoying themselves so much that they didn't have time to get nervous about their own performance.

Suddenly it was time to get ready. The sun was low in the sky, and the scene was set for Willow Shakespindle's *A Midsummer's Daydream*. The cast was ready and waiting backstage. Everyone was dressed in beautiful costumes – and they were all now very nervous.

The music started, the curtain went up, and Scarlet Larkspur stepped on to the stage to announce the play.

Here goes, thought Peri. She winked at her friends.

The actors took their places. Poppy was relieved to spot her mum and Heather in the audience, although she would never have admitted it.

The story unfolded. It was a magical tale of love and betrayal in fairyland. Peri was Tilia, the Fairy Queen, who had fallen in love with a prince who didn't love her back. So the queen asked Poppy's character, Bogbean, to help her. Bogbean agreed, but being a cheeky imp, made the prince fall in love with *her* instead of the queen! Bogbean and the prince made a ridiculous couple, and the audience were soon in stitches, laughing at Bogbean's silly pranks. Poppy was perfect for the part.

Then came the ballet – the moment Nina had been waiting for. At least we can help the actors win the competition, she thought. I'm going to dance like I've never danced before!

Nina and Bella twirled on to the stage. They danced up to the prince, skipping and jumping into entrechats: they jumped directly upwards, their

bodies straight, their feet changing position quickly, one in front of the other in mid-air. Their arms were stretched daintily above them. They whirled around the prince like leaves in the wind, as if to make him dizzy. He fell to the floor and was soon under the spell of the fairy ballerinas as they pirouetted around him. They gently waved their arms over him as if they were saying some secret magic words.

The dance was captivating. The audience waited with bated breath to see what these charming creatures had done to the prince. Nina and Bella ended their dance with the most delicate of curtseys.

Was that OK? Nina wondered.

The prince awoke from his enchantment and realized what Bogbean had done to him. When he saw what a fool he'd been, he rushed to ask the Fairy Queen for her forgiveness.

The play ended happily with a royal

wedding, and the audience leaped to their feet, cheering and applauding, their wings whirring with excitement.

"You've done it, guys!" Peri shouted above the noise as the fairies came to take their bows. "If we win this competition, it'll be down to you two!"

Nina grinned. Typical Peri, she thought, always thinking of her friends first.

The judges had gone back to their tent to discuss which act deserved the prize. Peri was so jittery that Nina suggested they all go and grab a drink while they waited for the announcement. They flittered to the refreshments tent and each ordered a frothy wild-strawberry milkshake.

"Hey! Look at me." Poppy tried to distract Peri by blowing froth everywhere and covering her own face in it so she looked like a little bearded gnome.

She looked ridiculous, but Peri could

only laugh half-heartedly. This competition meant so much to her. It was my idea to put the dance into the play, she thought. What if it was a mistake?

At last the judges flew back to the stage. The scary one with the monocle waited until everyone was silent and then spoke.

"I must say that the standard at this year's competition has made it harder than ever to judge who should win," she began. "However, my colleagues and I have observed everyone's contributions very closely and we are unanimous in our decision. And so it gives me great pleasure to present this year's Award for Excellence in the Fairy Arts to . . . the cast of *A Midsummer's Daydream!*"

"Yippee!" Peri shrieked, fluttering into the air. She felt as if she was floating on the applause.

"Hurray! Excellence in Airy Farts!" Poppy was shouting. Luckily the audience's clapping and cheering drowned out this last comment.

The judge handed a gleaming trophy to Scarlet Larkspur. Then she turned to Nina, Peri and Bella and called for silence.

"I have one thing to add," she announced. "The judges have decided that these three fairies deserve a special award. Nina Dewdrop and Bella Glove were to have performed in the ballet section of the competition but, as we all know, this had to be cancelled. However, their friend Periwinkle Moonshine saved the day!" The crowd started murmuring, but the judge carried on: "These three were not to be beaten! Nina and Bella joined in with the drama group only *last night* to put together their dance. And so I am delighted to be able to present them with these medals for Outstanding Achievement in the Fairy Arts. Well done, fairies!"

Nina had tears streaming down her face as she accepted her medal from the judge. Mrs Dewdrop and Heather made their way up on to the stage to congratulate the fairies. Then Nina held hands with Peri, Poppy and Bella and the four of them went to take their final bow.

"You were right, Bella. We did win the competition – with flying colours!" Nina said, beaming.

"Yeah, we beat that cheat all right!" Bella cried, punching the air in a most unfairylike manner.

"But you know what's more

important than winning, Nina," Peri said, hugging her friend. "Winning *together*!"

"Yeah," Poppy agreed, yelling above the rapturous applause, "and if it hadn't been for that old toad Cellophane Rosebum we never would've had the chance!"

Mrs Dewdrop opened her mouth to object to her younger daughter's rudeness, but she was beaten to it by Poppy's giggling friends, who chorused:

"POPPY, REALLY!"

Collect three tokens and get this gorgeous Nina Fairy Ballerina ballet bag!

There's a token at the back of each Nina Fairy Ballerina book
- Collect three tokens, and you can get your very own,
totally FREE Nina Fairy Ballerina ballet bag.

Send your three tokens, along with your name, address and
parent/guardian's signature
(you must get your parent/guardian's permission to take part in this offer)
to: Nina Fairy Ballerina Ballet Bag Offer, Marketing Department,
Macmillan Children's Books, 20 New Wharf Road, London N1 9RR

Nina Fairy Ballerina
Bag Offer

1 Token

Collect 3 tokens and get your free ballet bag!
Valid until 31/12/06

A selected list of titles available from Macmillan Children's Books

The prices shown below are correct at the time of going to press. However, Macmillan Publishers reserves the right to show new retail prices on covers, which may differ from those previously advertised.

ANNA WILSON

NINA FAIRY BALLERINA New Girl	ISBN-13: 978-0-330-43985-5 ISBN-10: 0-330-43985-5	£3.99
NINA FAIRY BALLERINA Daisy Shoes	ISBN-13: 978-0-330-43986-2 ISBN-10: 0-330-43986-3	£3.99
NINA FAIRY BALLERINA Best Friends	ISBN-13: 978-0-330-43987-9 ISBN-10: 0-330-43987-1	£3.99
NINA FAIRY BALLERINA Show Time	ISBN-13: 978-0-330-43988-6 ISBN-10: 0-330-43988-X	£3.99
NINA D	44620-4	£3.99

3Q

Fax: 01624 670923
Email: bookshop@enterprise.net
www.bookpost.co.uk

Free postage and packing in the United Kingdom